No Safe Trail

A Jackson Brooks Origin Story

PJ Mouchet

Paul Mouchet Publishing

Contents

Chapter One

A Frosty Greeting

The wipers squeaked against the windshield as Jackson guided his worn Suburban through the morning mist. Ruby's golden head appeared over his left shoulder, her warm breath fogging the glass as she watched the world through the driver's side window. Her excitement was palpable—she always knew when it was a working day.

"Ready for your big test, girl?" Jackson asked, reaching back to scratch behind her ear. The Golden Retriever's tail thumped against the leather seat in response. Six months of intensive tracking training had led to this moment, building upon her already-certified Search and Rescue skills. Jackson knew some of the other handlers thought he was crazy for pursuing a dual certification, but he'd seen Ruby's potential from day one. He knew SSA Frost was going to ratchet up the difficulty level, doing everything he could to make them fail.

The sign for Cheaha State Park emerged from the light fog, and Jackson turned onto the access road. Above them, Cheaha Mountain rose like a sentinel through the mist, its peak obscured by heavy clouds that promised the afternoon thunderstorm the weather service had been warning about. Ancient forests flanked the road, their branches swaying in the strengthening wind.

Jackson checked his dashboard clock—8:27 AM. He'd wanted to arrive even earlier, but morning traffic on I-20 had other ideas. Still, the email had clearly stated testing would begin at 9:00 AM. That gave them plenty of time to prepare.

The parking lot was nearly empty when they pulled in, just three other vehicles scattered across the asphalt. Jackson recognized Supervisory Special Agent Travis Frost's black Tahoe immediately. The senior trainer was already standing beside it, arms crossed, looking as welcoming as the storm clouds in the distance. The other two vehicles, a beat-up RAV4 and a gleaming silver Range Rover, sat empty and silent.

"Come on, Ruby," Jackson said, opening the back door. The Golden Retriever leaped out, her nose immediately going to work as she sampled the morning air. Her training vest caught the weak sunlight, FBI K-9 UNIT bold against the black material.

"You're late." Frost's voice carried across the parking lot before Jackson had even closed his door. The senior agent started walking toward them, each step radiating disapproval.

Jackson double-checked his watch. "Sir, the email said testing begins at nine. I'm thirty minutes early."

"The exam begins at nine. Orientation started at eight." Frost's face might as well have been carved from the mountain stone behind him. "Since you're late, you're not going to receive a full briefing."

Funny how I missed that 'nuance.' Not really.

Jackson felt heat rise in his neck, but his momma hadn't raised him to show disrespect to his superiors—even to those who seemed determined to see him fail. He forced a smile. "I apologize for the misunderstanding, sir. I must have—"

Ruby's sharp bark cut through the tension. Before either man could react, she bounded across the parking lot toward the Range Rover. Jackson's heart sank. This wasn't the way to start her final certification exam. But before he could call her back, Ruby had already snatched something from beside the luxury vehicle—a small blue stuffed bunny.

"Drop it!" Frost bellowed, but Ruby ignored him completely.

Frost didn't acknowledge the bunny was a part of the test, and Jackson hadn't expected him to. If it was, admitting it would only make things easier. And Frost wanted the opposite.

"Ruby, come," Jackson called, keeping his voice calm and firm. The Golden Retriever trotted back immediately, proudly carrying her find. When she reached Jackson, she sat and offered up the toy without hesitation. Jackson took it, noticing the way the fabric was damp with morning dew. It must have been there for a while.

SSA Frost's scowl deepened. "If you can't control your dog..."

"She's showing perfect recall, sir," Jackson interrupted, immediately regretting his boldness. But he couldn't help defending Ruby—especially since he suspected the bunny was part of the test. Target scenting was a crucial component of tracking, after all, and fundamentally different from SAR work.

"Let's get on with it," Frost said, turning toward the RAV4. "Here's your scenario. SA Hough will be playing the role of an escaped convict, considered armed and dangerous. He carjacked that vehicle and came up here to evade pursuit. We had to call off the search last night due to weather conditions. The high winds and heavy rain grounded all air support. The suspect's got a twelve-hour head start, and with this forest cover, drones and helicopters would be useless. We've got three other tracking teams coming in from different directions, doing what we can to box him in." He gestured at the RAV4. "Find something with the suspect's scent and get to work."

Jackson's heart sank as he processed the parameters. Last night's storm had likely washed away most of the trail. Twelve hours was an eternity in tracking time, and with another storm bearing down, their window was impossibly small. He glanced at the mountain where the clouds were growing darker by the minute.

The weather service had predicted the storm would hit around 6:00 PM, but looking at those clouds, he wouldn't be surprised if it came much earlier.

Still, he knew these mountains better than most. The terrain was harsh and unforgiving—doubly so in bad weather. With last night's storm, Jackson suspected Hough might not have gotten as far as Frost had hoped. Anyone unfamiliar with the area would have needed to seek shelter.

"Your time starts now," Frost announced, already turning away. "I'm no longer available to answer questions." He looked northward, where the clouds were darkest. "If you haven't secured your quarry before the thunderstorm hits, you fail."

Jackson watched him stride back to the Tahoe, then looked down at Ruby, who sat alert and ready at his feet.

"Well, girl, it looks like they've stacked the deck against us. But that's okay. We like a challenge, don't we?"

Ruby's tail wagged once, her eyes focused and bright. Even with Frost's unfair parameters, the washed-out trail, the looming storm, and the SSA's obvious bias—Jackson felt a surge of confidence. He and Ruby had trained for months, pushing through every obstacle thrown their way. Ruby had earned her SAR certification despite her young age, and she'd earn this one too.

The wind picked up, bringing with it the scent of pine and approaching rain. Jackson stood, still holding the blue bunny while staring back at Frost's Tahoe and watching the SSA sip his coffee. He hadn't missed how Frost had failed to mention the stuffed animal or the Range Rover in his briefing. There was more going on here than a certification test, but that was a puzzle for later. Right now, he and Ruby had a job to do.

"Let's go find our suspect, Ruby. Show them what dual certification really looks like."

After carefully sealing the blue bunny in an evidence bag, Jackson approached the RAV4, pleased to find it unlocked. A quick search revealed exactly what he needed—an orange prison shirt wadded up in the back seat. He quickly bagged it and jogged back to his Suburban with Ruby bouncing at his heels, her enthusiasm undiminished by Frost's hostility.

Jackson gathered his gear and slipped on his FBI vest over his T-shirt. With the impending weather, he considered putting on his raincoat, but he feared he'd overheat once he started running. After stowing it in his backpack, he holstered his Glock service pistol and slung a hunting rifle over his shoulder. Even though it was just a test, he wanted to be geared up like it was the real thing. Besides, there was a real possibility of running into bears or bobcats.

He adjusted the strap of his backpack and reached for his radio, pressing the button to confirm his frequency. A brief crackle of static. "Radio check," Jackson said.

"Try not to shoot SA Hough—not that you'll find him." Even over the radio, the senior agent's voice dripped with disdain. "And put a leash on your dog. I don't want to have to send out a real team to find her if she gets lost."

Jackson ignored the barbed comments and clipped the radio back onto his vest.

"My boss is an ass, isn't he girl?" he murmured to Ruby. He was completely secure in his trust in his K9's abilities. He'd been training dogs since he was a boy, guided by his mother's expertise as a professional trainer. Outside of his best friend, and fellow FBI agent, Tanner Montgomery, Jackson had always felt more at home with animals than people. People broke promises and played angles. Dogs never did that, unless you counted the occasional mealtime manipulation, like pretending you had forgotten to feed them. At two years old, Ruby was exceptionally young for an FBI SAR K-9, but she'd proven herself extraordinary in every way that mattered.

Ready to begin, Jackson pulled the orange shirt from its evidence bag and presented it to Ruby. "Find him," he commanded.

Ruby darted back to the RAV4, following the trail. She moved toward the north end of the parking lot, then stopped, spinning in slow circles that might have worried a less experienced handler. When she turned back to Jackson, he simply repeated the command: "Find him."

His faith was rewarded. Ruby returned to the RAV4, nose pinned to the ground as she worked the area more thoroughly. Suddenly, she let out an excited yip and turned west. Jackson smiled. The suspect had tried to throw them off with a false trail, doubling back before heading west into the wilderness. It was a clever trick, but not clever enough to fool Ruby.

Chapter Two

False Trails

Ruby moved with purpose through the dense forest, examining the ground in a zigzag pattern, telling Jackson that she had a solid scent trail. He kept her in sight but gave her room to work, only occasionally giving a quiet "Easy" command when she ranged too far ahead. The morning mist still clung to the lower branches of the pines, and Jackson's boots left deep impressions in the rain-softened earth.

The forest was a mix of old growth and new, towering pines interspersed with oak and birch. The terrain grew steadily more challenging as they moved west, the gentle slope becoming steeper with each passing minute. Jackson kept one eye on Ruby and one on their surroundings, noting landmarks they passed. Years of experience in these mountains had taught him the importance of maintaining situational awareness. Getting lost would be embarrassing enough on a normal day, but during a certification test, it would be unforgivable.

Ruby paused at the base of a massive oak, her nose working overtime as she circled the trunk. Their quarry had likely emptied his bladder here. Even with the heavy rain, Ruby could detect traces of urine.

"Good girl," Jackson murmured as Ruby picked up the trail again. She acknowledged his praise with a quick tail wag but stayed focused on her work. Her tracking was textbook perfect—head low, tail high, moving in a systematic pattern that would make any K-9 trainer proud. Some handlers thought mixing SAR and tracking training would confuse a dog, but Ruby was proving them wrong with every step.

The sound of rushing water grew louder as they approached a stream that cut through their path. Jackson knew this watershed well. It was normally just a gentle creek, but the recent rains had transformed it into a legitimate obstacle. The water churned brown and angry, carrying broken branches and debris from upstream.

Ruby stopped at the water's edge, and Jackson watched her body language carefully. This was a crucial moment. How she handled this challenge would say a lot about her training. Some dogs would lose the scent here, especially with the water running high and fast, contaminating the area with new smells and washing away old ones.

She worked the bank methodically, moving fifty yards upstream before turning back. Then she checked just as far downstream, her nose never leaving the ground. Jackson recognized what she was doing, checking to see if their quarry had entered and exited the water to mask his trail, just as he'd attempted in the parking lot. But Ruby wasn't fooled. She returned to their original crossing point with confident purpose. Ruby plunged into the stream without hesitation.

The water reached her chest, and she powered through, fighting the current with strong, steady strokes. Jackson followed. The shocking cold of the thigh-deep water stole his breath as he struggled to keep his footing on the uneven riverbed. Their quarry had likely crossed in the dark before last night's storm, before the trickle had become a raging torrent.

On the far bank, Ruby shook herself vigorously, then immediately dropped her nose back to the ground. She immediately picked up the trail and climbed the bank that rose sharply away from the water, forming a ravine that would test their endurance.

Jackson took a moment to catch his breath and check his watch. They'd been moving for almost forty-five minutes, making good time. Above them, the cloud cover had thickened, and the wind was picking up. The storm was moving faster than predicted.

The ravine was proving to be as demanding as it looked. The slope was steep enough that Jackson had to use saplings and exposed roots as handholds to haul himself up. Ruby scrambled ahead, her claws finding purchase in the soft earth. Through the difficult terrain she never lost focus on her task, only pausing to confirm the scent trail.

About halfway up, Ruby's behavior changed subtly. She was still tracking, but her pattern had shifted. Jackson studied her movements carefully. The trail was becoming more deliberate here, as if their quarry was planning something. Given that this was SA Hough, an extremely skilled and competent tracker, Jackson's suspicion grew. Like when he urinated against the tree, he had intentionally left an easy-to-find scent trail.

They were nearing the top of the ravine when Ruby stopped short. Her head lifted from the ground, testing the air instead of the earth. Jackson felt a flutter of concern. This was typical SAR behavior, not tracking. Had she lost the scent? Or worse, had her SAR training kicked in, overriding their current objective?

"Ruby, find him," Jackson commanded, ignoring his growing unease. Something wasn't right here, but he couldn't put his finger on exactly what.

Ruby's head remained high, testing the air currents that swirled around them. Without warning, she veered sharply to the right, abandoning the trail they'd been following for the past forty-five minutes. The sudden change in direction sent a jolt of concern through Jackson. This wasn't tracking behavior. This was pure SAR work, following an airborne scent rather than a ground trail.

"Ruby, find him," Jackson commanded again, more firmly this time. The last thing he needed was for her to switch disciplines in the middle of her certification test. What if she'd caught the scent of a hiker? Maybe it was the owner of the Range Rover? Perhaps she had picked up traces of whomever had left that blue bunny behind? The stuffed toy had been suspicious from the start, and now...

Ruby ignored his command, moving with increasing urgency through the dense underbrush. Her tail was high and tight, signaling she was onto something big. Jackson hesitated for half a second. She'd been locked onto Hough's track—so why the sudden shift? Then it hit him. She hadn't lost the trail. She'd found a fresher one.

He pushed through a thicket of mountain laurel, thorns catching at his clothes. The forest had grown denser here, old-growth trees creating a canopy that left the forest floor in perpetual twilight. Branches creaked overhead as the strengthening wind continued to announce the approaching storm.

A sharp bark echoed through the trees—Ruby's alert that she'd found her quarry. Jackson crashed through the remaining undergrowth, one hand instinctively moving to his holstered Glock. The scene that greeted him stopped him cold.

Ruby sat at attention beneath a massive oak, her eyes fixed upward. Following her gaze, Jackson spotted a figure perched casually on a thick limb about twelve feet up. The standard-issue FBI rain gear was impossible to miss, as was the familiar face beneath the hood.

"That's low," Jackson said, heat rising in his throat, "I'm guessing Frost put you up to this."

SA Kate Billingsley, Hough's partner, smiled down at him, looking entirely too pleased with herself. "Sorry, Brooks," she said, her tone making it clear she was anything but sorry. "Unlike you, I do what I'm told." She pulled out her cell phone and shrugged.

"Hey, boss. He took the bait, just like you expected. The dog doesn't know how to follow a scent trail."

Jackson's jaw tightened as he listened to her side of the conversation. The setup was clever, he had to admit. But it was also a cheap shot, designed to deliberately mislead Ruby and discredit her abilities. The pieces clicked into place.

"I'm guessing you came out this morning," Jackson said, keeping his voice level, hiding his growing anger. "And I'm guessing that's Hough's jacket you're wearing. Of course his scent is on you, and of course it's going to be stronger than last night's trail."

The agent smiled down at Jackson, confirming his suspicions.

The jacket's scent would be fresh and strong, exactly what Ruby was trained to follow in SAR scenarios. Frost had forced Ruby to make a choice—and whichever choice she made, he'd say it was the wrong one.

Jackson crossed his arms, studying her smug expression. "What time did your partner come through yesterday?"

Billingsley's smile widened as she settled more comfortably on her perch. "I'm the carjacking hostage," she announced with mock gravity. "The convict killed me, so I can't answer any questions." She made a show of checking her watch. "You and your dog are going to fail."

The wind gusted through the canopy, bringing with it the first spatters of rain. This wasn't the main storm, but rather the cold front that was moving ahead of it. They were running out of time, but Jackson refused to let that rush him into making a mistake.

He studied the scene, letting his training take over. Billingsley's position was well-chosen, upwind from their original trail, allowing her partner's scent to carry across their path. Ruby, doing exactly what she was supposed to do in SAR scenarios, had naturally investigated the stronger, fresher scent. The fact that she'd been able to differentiate between the old trail and the new scent actually demonstrated her exceptional abilities, though Frost would never see it that way.

The whole thing stank of manipulation. The falsified trail in the parking lot, Billingsley lying in wait with Hough's scent-laden clothing, even the time pressure of the approaching storm. Every element had been designed to make Ruby fail, to prove Frost's point about dual certification being impossible.

Jackson could have argued. He could have pointed out how Ruby's SAR training had allowed her to detect the target scent by any means available. Could have explained how this very scenario proved the value of having a dog trained in multiple disciplines.

His momma hadn't raised him to waste breath on people who wouldn't listen, but Jackson wasn't going to let this slide. This wasn't a mistake on Ruby's part. It was a deliberate and unrealistic trap to confuse his dog. It had cost Jackson some precious time, time he didn't have. One way or another, Frost was going to see them fail, and for what? Because Jackson had been moved to the K9 program without the SSA's consent? Jackson hadn't asked for special treatment, but when his SAC gave him the opportunity, he wasn't going to pass it up.

Jackson turned away from Billingsley and retraced their steps. A sharp whistle brought Ruby immediately to heel, her fluid transition from SAR alert to disciplined tracking dog a reflection of her amazing skills. Once she fell into position beside him, Jackson repeated the command. "Find him."

Ruby's response was immediate and decisive. She shot forward, returning unerringly to where she'd left the original trail, her nose dropping back to the ground as she resumed her pursuit of their true quarry. No hesitation, no confusion, just pure, professional focus. She had a solid track again, following the actual trail left by Hough the night before.

Behind them, Jackson heard Billingsley's voice carrying through the trees. "It's looks like he's back on the trail, Boss. He's not giving up."

The wind was picking up now, driving the rain sideways through the trees. Thunder rolled in the distance, closer than Jackson would have liked. With Billingsley's little diversion, and the storm bearing down on them, likely four hours ahead of schedule, the margin for error had shrunk to nothing.

If they didn't locate Hough soon, Jackson would have to make a call. Pushing deeper into the mountains with a storm this size on their heels wasn't just dangerous, it was deadly. He needed to find the trail, fast, or figure out a fallback point before they got trapped.

But Ruby showed no signs of doubt or distraction as she worked, her movements continuing to be precise and purposeful even through the deteriorating weather.

Jackson smiled grimly as they pushed forward. Let Frost and Billingsley play their games. Ruby had just proven exactly why he'd pushed for dual certification. She could switch between disciplines seamlessly, maintaining her tracking focus even after identifying and investigating a SAR target.

A fresh gust of wind brought another roll of thunder, closer this time. Ruby was already moving faster, as if sensing the urgency of their situation. Her nose never left the ground as she threaded through the trees, following a trail that only she could detect.

Jackson checked his watch, mentally calculating distances. The *convict*, Hough, couldn't be too far ahead of them. Frost had said there were other search parties, which would technically limit how far Hough could move. Knowing where every other entry point was, Jackson determined that their prey had likely gone to the most inaccessible location in the park—the northwest side of the mountain. The terrain was particularly rugged, and that side of the mountain was too steep to traverse without specialized gear. They were going to find him. Ruby would pass this test, and in doing so, she'd prove every doubter wrong.

Jackson barely had time to pull out his rain jacket before the sky split open. Fat raindrops broke through the canopy to pepper the forest floor, a warning of what was to come. Jackson glanced up, watching the sky continue to darken much faster than expected.

Ruby didn't even seem to notice; her focus absolute as she tracked.

Chapter Three

A Cry for Help

The downpour struck with crushing force, piercing the canopy and overwhelming his FBI-issued rain gear in seconds. Ruby pressed against his leg, her body tense. The ground, still saturated from last night's storm, shed the water in sheets. Within seconds, tiny rivulets formed around his boots, carrying loose pine needles and debris downhill.

"Ruby, heel." The young Golden Retriever obeyed instantly, her training overriding her instinct to seek cover.

Jackson kept one hand on Ruby's head, both for her comfort and his own. The roar of rain on leaves made it impossible to hear anything else, creating a temporary sensory isolation that set his nerves on edge. Through the curtain of water, he could barely make out trees fifteen feet away. If SSA Frost had planned this weather as part of his test, Jackson had to admire the tactical precision. The rain would not only obscure their target's trail but also mask any sound that might give away planted distractions.

The deluge lasted barely three minutes, but its effects transformed the landscape. As quickly as it had arrived, the rain ceased, leaving behind a forest that seemed to exhale steam as sunshine broke through the clouds. Wind whipped through the canopy, sending cascades of collected rainwater down in sporadic showers. The immediate problem wasn't the rain itself, but what it had done to the terrain. Every depression had become a pool, every slope a potential slide, and the nearby stream—which had been running high but manageable—now roared with fresh runoff from higher elevations.

"Alright, girl," Jackson murmured, releasing Ruby from heel position. "Show me what momma taught us about wet conditions."

Ruby needed no further encouragement. She immediately dropped her nose, quartering the area where they'd left off. Jackson watched her body language, noting how she adjusted her tracking technique for the rain-altered scent pattern. His mother had spent countless hours training them for exactly these conditions, teaching Ruby to account for how water would affect scent distribution and teaching Jackson to read the subtle changes in his partner's behavior.

The Golden Retriever's tail lifted slightly—her tell for picking up the trail. Instead of following the scent cone in a straight line as she typically would, Ruby began working in a weaving pattern, compensating for how the rain had scattered their quarry's scent. Jackson followed, paying careful attention to his footing on the slick ground. The forest floor had become treacherous, with mud concealing loose rocks and roots.

They made slower progress than they had before the rain, but Jackson felt a surge of pride watching Ruby work. Most dogs would have lost the trail completely in these conditions. The fact that she maintained it while simultaneously adapting her technique validated every hour they'd spent training. He could almost hear his mother's voice: "A dog that can track through rain can track through anything, but only if their handler trusts them enough to listen to what they're saying."

Ruby led them along a narrow game trail that skirted the edge of the increasingly swollen stream. The water level had risen notably in just a few minutes since the rain, carrying a heavy load of silt that turned it the color of coffee with too much cream. Jackson kept one eye on the rushing water, all too aware of how quickly mountain streams could rise after rain.

The wind continued to gust, causing the wet branches overhead to shed their burden in sudden showers. These sporadic soakings were more annoying than dangerous, but they forced Jackson to remain vigilant. Every unexpected splash of water made him flinch, each one a potential distraction that could mask a more serious threat.

They had covered perhaps a quarter mile when Ruby's ears suddenly pricked forward. Jackson froze mid-step, listening intently. For a moment, all he could hear was the rush of water and the drip of rain from leaves. Then it came again—voices carried on the wind, coming from somewhere downstream.

Ruby's behavior changed instantly. The focused, methodical tracking posture vanished, replaced by the alert tension Jackson associated with her search and rescue training. She turned to look at him, then back toward the sound of voices, her body trembling with barely contained urgency.

Jackson's jaw tightened. The timing was too perfect, the situation too convenient. They were in the middle of a certification test, one SSA Frost designed to push them to failure. What were the odds that they would just happen to encounter a real emergency? This had to be another element of the test, another attempt to derail them from their primary objective.

But Ruby's behavior nagged at him. She was young for an FBI K9, yes, but she was also one of the most naturally gifted dogs he'd ever worked with. More importantly, she had been raised and trained by his mother, a woman who could read dogs better than most people could read books. If Ruby was showing this level of urgency, she wasn't just hearing voices, she was picking up something in those voices that demanded attention.

The calls came again, louder and clearer than before. Two distinct voices, carried on the wind that whipped through the trees. Jackson couldn't make out words yet, but there was a pitch to them that made the hair on his neck stand up.

Ruby whined softly, taking two steps toward the sound before looking back at him again. Her eyes held that intensity he'd seen countless times during SAR training, the look that said she'd found something that required their attention. But this was a tracking test, not a rescue scenario. If he diverted now, he risked failure.

A memory surfaced—his mother's voice, steady as ever. "The day you ignore what your dog is telling you is the day you should quit handling. The dog doesn't care about tests, son. The dog only cares about what's right."

The voices came again, closer now. Ruby whined—no hesitation, no doubt. She knew. She always knew.

Damn the test.

Jackson exhaled, decision made. "Okay, girl," he murmured. "Seek."

Ruby took point immediately, but not at her usual tracking pace. She moved deliberately, choosing each step with unusual care as they descended the steep hillside. The stream beside them had grown into a churning mass of brown water, carrying broken branches and debris from higher ground. Every few yards, Ruby would pause and look back, making sure Jackson was navigating the treacherous terrain safely.

The voices grew clearer as they descended. A man and woman, their calls overlapping with increasing desperation: "Peggy! Baby, where are you? Peggy!"

Jackson's tactical training kicked in as they rounded a bend in the hillside. He cataloged details automatically: two civilians approximately thirty yards downstream, no visible weapons, body language consistent with extreme distress. The woman's hands were cupped around her mouth as she called, while the man paced in short, agitated bursts along the fast-flowing stream bank.

The woman's next shout died in her throat as she spotted Jackson and Ruby. The man spun toward them with the jerky movement of someone operating on pure adrenaline. They rushed forward, splashing through puddles and sliding on wet leaves in their haste.

"Oh, thank God," the woman cried out. "Please, are you with the park service? Police? Our niece... Oh Jesus, we can't find her. She's only six."

Chapter Four

Missing

"FBI," Jackson said, holding up his badge. Ruby shifted her weight forward, ears flicking toward the couple. Her body tensed—not in fear, but in focus. She was picking up on something—whether it was their distress or something else, Jackson wasn't sure yet.

"I'm Special Agent Jackson Brooks. What do you mean you can't find her? Who exactly are you looking for?" He groaned inwardly, expecting that this was all a part of the test, designed to distract him from the manhunt he was supposed to be conducting. But, in his mind, it didn't matter. A missing child took priority over an escaped convict and if Frost didn't agree... well, he'd deal with that later.

The man grabbed his wife's arm, either for support or to stop her headlong rush toward them. "Our niece," he said, his voice cracking. "Her name's Peggy. She was playing by the stream. I swear, we only left her for a minute, and then we heard the rush of water."

Jackson's jaw tightened. "You left a six-year-old alone by this stream?" The water was deep, fast, and extremely dangerous for a child of any age. He forced himself to keep his voice level. "Tell me exactly what happened."

"The stream wasn't like this before," the uncle added quickly. "It was just a little thing, barely ankle deep. But now..." He gestured helplessly at the swollen waterway. "There must have been runoff from the mountain... We started following the stream from our camp, fearing our niece got swept away."

"When exactly did you last see her?" Jackson kept his tone professionally neutral, but his mind was racing, trying to piece everything together.

"Maybe twenty minutes ago?" The woman looked to her husband for confirmation. "Before the rain started. She was looking for salamanders. She loves salamanders. She had her little pink bucket..." Her voice broke. "We were..."

"You were what?" Jackson asked. The story didn't sound like a training exercise. It was too convoluted, and there was no way they could have planned for the torrential downpour that had happened only minutes earlier.

"We're here birdwatching," the woman said, her voice raw with guilt. "We belong to a group of enthusiasts... There's a list of birds we need to photograph before the end of the month. We're only two birds behind the leader." She swallowed hard. "We told Peggy to stay put and that we were nearby, but I guess we got distracted trying to get a shot of a peregrine falcon. When we looked back, she was gone." Her voice broke. "We should have been watching her better."

Bile rose in Jackson's gut. These idiots had likely left the child much longer than a few minutes, and she could have easily wandered off rather than having been swept away by the stream.

Jackson scanned their faces, searching for any sign of deception. He saw none. The woman's mascara was streaked down her cheeks, her hands shaking as she pushed wet hair from her face. The man's complexion had the gray undertone of genuine fear, and there was mud on his hands and the knees of his jeans where he'd clearly been scrambling along the bank.

Ruby hadn't moved from her alert position, her attention fixed on the tree line beyond the stream.

"Show me exactly where you last saw her," Jackson said.

The couple led them a short distance upstream to a small clearing. A makeshift camp had been erected with a canopy tent, two collapsible chairs, and a propane heater. Jackson moved past the camp to the stream. On any other day, this would have been the perfect spot for a child—gentle slopes, flat rocks for hopping across the water. Now, those same rocks were nearly invisible beneath the churning current, swallowed by the storm's runoff. Jackson's eye caught something in the mud near one of the larger rocks. "Ruby, stay," he commanded, then turned to the parents. "You, too."

He crouched to examine the ground, mentally filtering out the recent rain damage. There were multiple footprints preserved in the softer earth, including small ones that had to be Peggy's. But what caught his attention was a larger print, deeply set as if made by someone carrying extra weight. Jackson's breath caught. The tread pattern was wrong. Deep, angular grooves. Raised arch. Not a hiker's boot. Not a trail runner. This was a boot designed for tactical movement—fast, silent, built for long distances in rough terrain.

A chill settled in his gut.

"Sir," Jackson called to the uncle, keeping his voice even. "Would you mind showing me the bottom of your boots?"

The man complied immediately, lifting each foot. His boots were well-worn Merrells with a completely different tread pattern. Jackson felt his stomach tighten. This was likely an abduction, and time was against them.

"What's wrong?" the aunt said, her voice breaking—high, raw, the kind of sound that only true terror could produce. "Why are you checking Bernie's boots?"

Ruby whined softly, her eyes locked on his. In that moment, Jackson made his decision. Certification be damned. A child's life came first. Static crackled as he pressed his radio mic.

"Giving up already?" Frost said with a sarcastic laugh. "Did a little rain shake your confidence?"

"Did you plant this couple?" Jackson said, disregarding his boss's taunting words. "Did you add a missing child to the scenario?"

"What are you babbling about, Agent?" Frost said, his previous dismissive tone had a new edge to it.

"I've come across a couple who said their niece is missing." He turned his back away from the aunt and uncle and lowered his voice. "If this isn't part of the test, I'm concerned that she's been abducted."

"Are you fucking with me, Brooks?" the SSA said. "Because if you are, I won't just fail you and your K9, I'll have you disciplined."

"I'm going to send you my pin," Jackson said. "Send Billingsley and get Hough to call me so that we can coordinate our positions."

"No need to send your location," Frost said. "I'm already tracking your cell phone. Text me photos of the couple's driver's licenses. I'm going to have background checks run on them."

"You do that," Jackson said. His boss wasn't wrong, but if this was an abduction, delaying wasn't an option. "I'm going to take Ruby and start the search."

"You'll wait until Billingsley gets there," Frost said. The tone in his voice left no room for objection. "We don't know who these people are, and you and your K9 are not tracking certified. I'll get actual K9 units out to your position as quickly as possible."

Jackson looked toward Cheaha Mountain. The peak was completely shrouded in dark clouds, and the wind carried the fresh scent of an impending storm.

"Negative. The forecast was wrong. That storm is going to hit in less than two hours. Look at the size of the cloud bank. It's going to hit us hard, and the rain will wipe the trail clean. We'll lose her. I'm leaving with Ruby now. If you don't like it, you can discipline me when we get back. The deep-set boot print wasn't from a casual hiker—it was the kind of footwear a serious outdoorsman would use. Whoever took Peggy was prepared to move through this terrain. Fast and light. I suspect he's an experienced woodsman, and he's already got a thirty-minute head start. If I'm right, I need to start tracking him right away."

Before Frost could respond, a thought occurred to Jackson. "Send local PD to the Cheaha State Park Campgrounds. It's the closest point from where we are that has road access. He might have a car waiting for him there. I figure it's about a 45-minute hike from here to there, so tell them to hurry."

"Go," Frost said. The edge in his voice had vanished, replaced with obvious concern. "Good luck."

Jackson straightened, his voice turning crisp, controlled. "Ma'am, sir, I need your ID."

"You're wasting time," the man said, his tone and body language turning belligerent. "Our niece is missing, and you want to interrogate us?"

The man's response wasn't out of line, but Jackson had no intention of explaining why his SSA wanted their details. "I'm concerned that your niece was abducted—"

"God, no!" the woman shrieked. She spun toward Bernie, gripping his arm hard enough to make him flinch. "Bernie... tell me this isn't about the money."

Bernie shook his head, his face etched with worry. "No... no, that's not possible. We didn't know Peggy was coming with us until your sister dropped her off at five this morning." The lines creasing Bernie's forehead deepened. "What if it's your sister's ex? What if the crazy sonofabitch followed us here?"

"Listen to me," Jackson bellowed. The reason for the abduction could wait. "Give me your ID so that the FBI can start their investigation. I'm going to give you my boss's number. Tell him everything that's happened, and don't you dare leave anything out."

Bernie nodded and retrieved his wallet from his back pocket. He pulled his driver's license and handed it to Jackson.

"My name's Eileen Runstedler, but I don't have any ID with me," the woman said. "My sister dumped her daughter on us this morning... Everything happened so fast, I forgot my wallet." Her eyes turned glassy and filled with tears. "My sister is going to hate me forever. What were we thinking, bringing a six year old out here?"

Jackson texted Bernie Runstedler's driver's license to SSA Frost, along with a quick note that the couple would be calling him shortly to provide details.

"Now," he said, turning to the distraught couple. "Tell me everything about Peggy. What she looks like, what she's wearing, and anything that might help Ruby track her."

"She's about this tall," Bernie said, holding his hand about waist high. "She's cute, with curly blonde hair and a round face. Her eyes are brown, I think."

"Blue," Eileen interjected. "Her eyes are blue. She's wearing a yellow slicker and pink boots. We don't have anything of hers. She had a blue bunny, but she dropped it along the trail."

Jackson laid his rifle on the ground and pulled off his backpack. He unzipped the top and pulled out the evidence bag containing the blue bunny. "Is this it? Is this her toy?"

Eileen nodded emphatically while tears streamed down her cheeks. "She never goes anywhere without it. She was inconsolable during the hike. She didn't stop until I gave her my iPhone to play games on."

"Does she still have it?" Jackson asked. "Does it have a tracking app enabled on it?"

"I think she still has it," Eileen said. "It's got GPS tracking turned on, so that we can record the route we take while birding. I don't know if that's what you mean."

Bernie pulled out his phone. "It's got a tracking app installed," he said, clicking frantically on his phone. "I never thought of checking." His voice carried a mix of excitement and regret, possibly for not having thought of it earlier. A frown pulled at his lips as he looked north across the stream. "The map says she's standing right there on the other side of the stream. She must have dropped it."

"It gives Ruby and I a starting direction," Jackson said, doing his best to sound hopeful. "Here's my boss's phone number. Call him now and tell him that Ruby and I are heading north towards Cheaha Mountain, in the opposite direction to the campground trailhead."

"Hello," Bernie said. "This is Bernie Runstedler. The agent told me to call you."

Jackson disregarded the conversation while he gave Ruby the stuffed animal to sniff. "Find her."

The K9's nose twitched as she snuffled at the toy, then pressed to the earth. A heartbeat later, she picked up the trail, moving sure and deliberate as she retraced the girl's footsteps. Jackson pulled on his backpack and threw his rifle over his shoulder.

The dog's head lifted, checking for Peggy's scent in the air currents.

"Ruby, seek!" Jackson switched to her SAR command.

"Ruby immediately jumped into the stream and Jackson gave chase. The swift water surged over his boots and pushed hard at his balance. He gritted his teeth and waded deeper.

The wind gusted, hard enough to rattle the trees. Thunder rolled, closer now. Time was running out.

Two hours, at most. That was all they had to find Peggy.

Or lose her forever.

Chapter Five

The Hunt

Ruby burst from the stream, water pouring from her coat as she pressed her nose to the ground. She hesitated for only a second before powering up the muddy bank, nose down, and locked onto the scent.

Jackson's stomach knotted. There. In the soft mud—the same heavy-tread boot pattern. And beside it, a tiny set of footprints, moving in parallel.

She was still walking.

The child's abductor was moving through rough terrain with a six-year-old in tow. That would slow him down, hopefully negating much of his head start.

The wet leaves and churned-up mud made the incline treacherous, forcing Jackson to dig his boots in with every step. His rifle bounced hard against his back, but he barely felt it. All that mattered were Ruby, the tracks ahead, and the shrinking window before Peggy's trail vanished forever.

The forest was thick here, the humid air pressing in like a heavy hand. Tree branches clawed at his sleeves as he passed, and the damp earth sucked at his boots. The storm wasn't here yet, but the scent of it clung to the air—wet earth, distant rain, the charge of the storm brewing on the horizon.

Ruby was locked in, nose low to the ground, body taut with determination. She weaved through the trees, her pace steady and sure. It had been several minutes since Jackson had seen any boot prints, but he had faith in his dog's skills. At the crest of a small knoll, Ruby stopped abruptly, looking back. Her big brown eyes weren't confused. They were troubled. Jackson pushed himself up the slope, breath sharp in his chest. When he reached her, he saw it.

A single, tiny pink boot.

Jackson's breath caught. The prints veered east—erratic, frantic. Small handprints, knee imprints. The earth was clawed up where she had struggled.

Atta girl. You fought and you ran. It wouldn't have saved her, but she was refusing to go down easy, and she had no intention of just giving in.

Ruby's head snapped to the right, picking up the fresh scent of Peggy's lost boot. She bolted ahead and snuffled at the footwear. She took a quick look for Jackson and tore through a thicket, disregarding the thorns and stiff branches. The underbrush was much too thick for Jackson, forcing him to take a longer route. Ruby let out a short, sharp alert bark and veered back toward the north. Jackson's heart kicked against his ribs as he caught up with Ruby beside an ancient pine tree.

"What do you have, girl?"

He crouched, scanning the ground around the massive trunk. And then he saw it—a great rent at the base; gnarled roots that formed a natural cave. A small muddy handprint, low on the bark of a tree, smeared and uneven. Jackson barely dared to hope. He crouched by the gnarled roots, peering into the hollow. If she was there, if she had managed to hide...

"Peggy, honey?" His voice was calm, but his pulse pounded. "Are you in there? I'm a friend of your Aunt Eileen. It's safe now. You can come out. I have your blue bunny."

Blood rushed in Jackson's ears as he waited for a response. If she was in the hole, she was too frightened to call back. "Peggy, you're safe. You can come out now."

Ruby barked, drawing Jackson's attention from the tree. She was looking west, clearly eager to continue moving. If Peggy was there, the K9 wouldn't have wanted to leave. His gut twisted, and the spark of hope in his chest snuffed out.

"Let's go," he said, rising to his feet. "Find her, Ruby."

She surged forward again, tail high, sniffing deep, and Jackson followed.

Jackson had barely caught his breath before Ruby shot north again, weaving through the trees like liquid gold. He forced himself to keep up, lungs burning from the humid air. The ground here was firmer, covered in tangled roots and pine needles, but he could still make out boot prints cutting east. Peggy's tiny one-booted tracks stayed beside them. She was still on foot.

Ruby charged into a narrow clearing. Then, without warning, she stopped. With her nose low, and paws churning up damp earth, she backtracked, snuffling the ground frantically. She looped the area once. Twice. Then she whined softly, confused.

Jackson's heart lurched. She'd lost the trail. He scanned the ground. No more small footprints. His gut turned to stone.

Peggy was off the ground.

Jackson forced himself to breathe. Focus. Analyze.

The boot prints were deeper, wider-spaced. He was moving faster, pushing harder. He was carrying her.

Jackson set his jaw. This wasn't panic. It was strategy. The abductor knew time was against him. He was moving faster now, but he'd also be burning more energy.

Ruby trotted in a tight circle, then backtracked again. Jackson knelt beside her, pressing a gentle hand to her back. "Here, girl," he said, pointing to the abductor's boot print. It wasn't much for her to go on, but, hopefully, it would be enough. "Ruby, find him."

She huffed, then surged ahead. Again, Jackson followed.

They hadn't gone another hundred yards before the ground sloped downward. In the distance, a rumble of thunder rolled across the land. The wind kicked up, sending leaves and forest debris skittering over the ground. A light drizzle pattered against his head. Over the noise, he heard it.

Jackson cursed under his breath at the sound of another rushing stream. If Peggy's abductor had been thinking ahead, this was exactly the kind of place he'd use to throw them off.

Ruby didn't hesitate—she bolted straight for the bank. Jackson pushed forward, boots slipping slightly in the wet loam beneath him. His boots lost traction, sending him sliding. He instinctively grabbed for a branch but, realizing he couldn't stop, twisted his body to control the descent. He hit the bottom hard—but he'd saved precious seconds.

The stream wasn't as deep or violent as the first, but it was wide and moved quickly. Large stones jutted from the water, slick and dark. Overhead, branches swayed in the rising wind.

Ruby whined. She sniffed frantically at the water's edge, then backpedaled, confused. She barked once, ears twitching. She wasn't just confused. She was uncertain. Her head was high, ears flicking constantly. Her tail moved in tiny, deliberate shifts, adjusting to the air currents.

The scent was gone.

Jackson scanned the area, his pulse hammering. No tracks leading out. No clear exit point.

The K9 moved upstream a few yards, her head and tail high. She let out a sharp bark, telling Jackson she'd found something. She stamped at the ground, desperate to run. She had picked up their scent again.

Jackson squinted at the stones barely protruding from water. Wet boot scuffs. The abductor was using the river to mask his tracks, but he had likely stumbled, forcing him to use the stone to maintain his balance. Jackson could practically see it in his mind: the bastard clutching Peggy in his arms, hopping between the rocks, doing everything he could to avoid leaving a scent trail.

"Go," Jackson yelled, urging Ruby to continue. "Find Peggy."

The dog obeyed. She bounded through the water and into the forest. The trees were dense ahead, the canopy swaying as the wind picked up. Without warning, the wind died off and the world suddenly felt too still, too quiet, and too dark. Jackson looked up. Dark clouds loomed overhead, stalled and heavy with rain.

At this point, Jackson didn't care if Ruby got out of eyesight. When she'd worked SAR, she often ran far ahead. She was faster and when she caught a scent, she needed to follow it before it disappeared. Jackson pulled out the dog whistle hanging around his neck. When he needed to, he knew he could call her back. Ruby's recall bordered on perfection.

Hiking his pack higher onto his back, Jackson gripped his rifle's shoulder strap and took off. He kept his eyes and ears sharp, doing what he could to follow Ruby's trail. If he couldn't hear her barking, he would look for other signs—footprints, broken branches, trampled grasses. There was always a trail if you knew what to look for. Jackson thanked his father for teaching him everything he knew about surviving in the woods. If Travis Brooks hadn't been a committed police officer, he could have been a trainer at Quantico—and they'd have been lucky to have him.

Ruby's frantic barks told Jackson that she was close. He put his head down and charged forward. A gunshot ripped through the trees, sharp and deafening. Jackson's heart stopped at the sound. A second shot cracked through the air, and his blood ran cold.

He was shooting at Ruby.

Fearing for his dog's life, Jackson pressed the whistle to his lips and blew a sharp blast. The sound was inaudible to humans, but Ruby could hear it from miles away.

Whether it was from exertion, or concern for his dog, Jackson's breathing and heart rate flew out of control. The world swam before him, as double vision blurred the trees. He didn't care. He would run until his heart exploded.

The Golden Retriever exploded from the trees, her eyes wide and bright. Jackson fell to his knees, overcome with relief. Ruby ran to his side, nudged him, and headed back to where she had come from.

Still winded and overcome with concern, Jackson hoisted himself back to his feet, pulled his rifle off his shoulder, and pressed on.

They ran for ten minutes before the howl of the wind ripped through the trees. It was the harbinger of the coming storm. The trees bent to the onslaught and the rain pattered through the leaves. A crack of lightning lit up the clouds just before the sky opened up and a deluge of rain dropped.

Peggy was nearby. Ruby had her scent. The weather would affect Peggy's abductor as much as it would Jackson. A grim smile crossed his lips. Then—

A metallic clank cut through the storm's howl. Jackson halted, listening hard through the wind and rain. The sound had come from beyond the trees, sharp and artificial. Then came another sound, a deep, mechanical roar beneath the storm. Jackson's breath caught as recognition hit.

Ruby barked sharply, her tail rigid.

He didn't hesitate. Jackson sprinted forward, his pulse slamming against his ribs. As he cleared the tree line, he caught sight of it... a four-wheeler, taillights glowing red in the rain, kicking up gravel as it sped away.

Over the ATV's roar and the storm's howl, Peggy screamed.

Chapter Six

On the Trail

Jackson yanked his radio from his vest. "Agent Hough, what's your position?" Static crackled through the speaker, mixing with the patter of rain through leaves. "Agent Hough, do you copy?"

"Brooks?" Hough's voice fought through the interference. "I'm about half a mile north of the ranger lookout. Heard shots. You okay?"

"I'm in pursuit of the kidnapper on an ATV. He's got a six-year-old girl."

"I heard," Hough answered. "What do you want me to do?"

Jackson's mind raced through the terrain's possibilities. The trail followed the mountain's natural contours, which meant there was a place up ahead to catch up with the ATV. "He's on Big Foot Trail heading towards the summit."

"Big Foot? He's looking to get on the Bunker Loop. He can get to multiple trailheads from there."

"We can't let him get there," Jackson said. "There's a switchback not far from here. Big Foot doubles back on itself before it makes the final climb to the summit. How close are you to the upper section?"

A pause. "Maybe four hundred yards. You want to cut him off?"

"If we time it right, we can box him in." Jackson adjusted his pack, shifting the weight higher on his shoulders. "But we've got to move fast."

"Copy that. Going radio silent unless emergency."

Ruby whined softly, her eyes locked on the trail where the ATV had disappeared. Jackson touched her head briefly. "I know, girl. We'll catch them."

The forest ahead was a mess of fallen trees and thick mountain laurel. The shortest distance between two points was a straight line—but in terrain like this, straight lines could get you killed. Jackson took a deep breath and slowly let it out. The ATV would have to follow the trail's path up to the switchback where it would turn 180 degrees and head back this way. In all, it was maybe 800 yards. If Jackson cut across through the forest, he could reach the trail above him in less than fifty yards. The trouble was, the slope up to the trail was incredibly steep in places. In this weather, and without ropes, he was going to need Ruby's help to make the ascent. He unhooked her leash from his pack and snapped it onto her harness.

"Let's go," he said. "Lead the way."

They plunged into the undergrowth. Thorns caught at Jackson's clothes as he pushed through the dense vegetation. The slope rose sharply. While Ruby pulled, he scrambled for any handhold to pull himself upward. His boots slipped on the wet leaves and muddy patches. On several occasions, Ruby lost her footing and had to scramble to not topple down the mountainside. He tightened his grip on the leather lead. He wouldn't let that happen.

Ruby moved ahead, keeping the leash taught. She seemed to understand the urgency of their mission, yet picked paths through the undergrowth that her human partner could follow.

The rain slowed to a drizzle but everything was already fully saturated. Water ran in rivulets down the steep slope, making the footing even more treacherous. Thunder growled in the distance, reminding him that the real storm was still to come.

Jackson's legs burned as he climbed. His chest heaved, trying to suck in more oxygen. Salty sweat mixed with the rain on his face. His rifle slammed against his back with every step, reminding him exactly what might be waiting at the top. His tactical training screamed at him to not make a direct ascent. It was too taxing. He feared neither of them would have enough energy to deal with the kidnapper when the time came. Ruby paused, her tongue lolling out the side of her mouth.

"Ruby, go!" he yelled, fearing he was pushing her beyond her limit.

The K9 lowered her head and powered forward. When Jackson's foot slipped out from beneath him, she was forced to carry his weight, to save them both from tumbling down the hillside. Once he recovered his footing, she soldiered on.

A fallen oak blocked their path, its massive trunk waist high. Ruby tried to climb over it, but she no longer had the strength. With her front paws scrambling for purchase, Jackson grabbed her rear end and hoisted her up. She stood on the massive log, waiting for her partner to catch up. Jackson threw himself, belly first, onto the tree and swung his legs over.

Ruby's chest was heaving uncontrollably now. Her eyes lacked the brightness they usually had.

"Stay," he said, unclipping her harness. He scratched the top of her head. "You rest here."

The roar of the ATV's engine broke the silent moment. The kidnapper had likely passed the switchback, leaving no time to rest.

"Stay," Jackson repeated and bolted up the slope. Before he made ten paces, Ruby chugged past him and disappeared over the ridge.

Stubborn dog.

Jackson should've known better—she wasn't going to sit this one out.

Ruby reappeared a moment later and unleashed a series of high-pitched barks. She looked to her right and barked again. The ATV was coming.

Energized by his dog, Jackson scrambled up the last few yards to the trail. His chest burned with each breath. Rain started to fall in earnest again. The water running over his head and down his back cooled his body, but it made it difficult to see up the trail.

"Come on, girl," he said, jogging toward the switchback. A gust of wind drove the rain in sideways sheets, pelting against Jackson's face like buckshot. The cloud cover thickened, plunging the late morning into near darkness.

A pinpoint of light appeared in the distance, perhaps four hundred yards away. Jackson positioned himself in the middle of the trail and pulled his rifle off his shoulder. He couldn't use it, not with the child on the ATV with the kidnapper, but hopefully it would be enough to give the unsub a reason to stop. The man was a monster, and he would think like a monster... the idea of sparing a child's life would never occur to him.

"Ruby, behind," he yelled. A shiver ran through Jackson's entire body. From her place, Ruby pressed her shoulder against his thigh, letting her partner know that she was with him.

The roar of the engine grew louder, its harsh beam of light brighter. Two hundred yards now.

Jackson lifted his rifle to his shoulder and flipped open the scope. At this range, he could end this right now—one clean shot. The single headlight blinded him, a wall of white slicing through the rain. He couldn't risk it.

Hopefully the kidnapper didn't know that.

Jackson's breath came in short, sharp bursts, his chest burning from the brutal climb. His pulse pounded in his ears, but he forced himself to focus as the ATV thundered towards him. The beam bounced with each jarring movement over the uneven trail. Ruby vibrated against his leg, her muscles coiled, waiting. The moment was coming.

Movement flickered to Jackson's right, and Agent Hough burst from the trees, positioning himself in the middle of the trail about fifty yards ahead. The ATV's engine roared as the driver gunned it, showing no signs of slowing.

"FBI! STOP!" Hough's voice carried over the engine noise and rain. He pulled his sidearm from its holster, leveled it at the unsub, and again bellowed for him to stop. Jackson's heart flew into his throat when Hough fired two shots in quick succession.

God, no!

The ATV swerved hard, its back-end fishtailing on the wet gravel. For a heart-stopping moment, Jackson thought the vehicle would plow straight into his fellow agent. Instead, it veered sharply right, catching the edge of the trail.

The driver yanked the handlebars—too late. The wheels hit loose ground, skidding sideways. For half a second, the ATV hung there, balanced between control and catastrophe.

Gravity won.

The vehicle flipped, headlights slashing through the darkness as it tumbled into the void. The roar of the engine cut off mid-scream, swallowed by the forest below. The gut-wrenching crashes followed. Metal crunching. Plastic snapping. Tree branches exploding under impact.

"No!" Jackson's throat burned with the cry as he sprinted forward. Ruby bolted ahead, but he grabbed her harness. "Heel!"

Hough followed the ATV, running headlong over the side.

Chapter Seven

Double Jeopardy

Jackson sprinted forward, searching for the point where the ATV had vanished. The high winds and pelting rain barely registered. All he could think about was the child, and the likelihood of her not having survived the crash. He wanted to thrash the agent for his reckless behavior, but that would have to wait.

Jackson spotted the skid marks in the gravel and rushed to the edge of the steep drop-off. It was too dark to see clearly, but he could make out Hough's silhouette as he picked his way down.

Two gunshots split the storm. Muzzle flashes flared like lightning, illuminating the trees for a fraction of a second. Hough staggered—then collapsed.

Jackson's throat tightened. His rifle was already up, but there was nothing to shoot—just shadows and swirling rain. Quickly, he slung it over his shoulder and drew his Glock.

"Stay close," he said to Ruby. "Don't you dare take off."

The wet ground would make the descent treacherous, but there was no time for caution. Leaning back on his heels, he went over the edge. At his side, Ruby did her best to control her descent. Her paws braced against the loose ground, but it was too slippery. A moment later, she was racing down the slope, leaving Jackson on his own. He wanted to call out, but he didn't know if the unsub was still close. All he could do was hope that she was okay.

"Brooks," a pained voice called through the pounding rain. "Down here."

"I'm coming," he called back. Jackson adjusted his angle of descent, heading towards Hough's voice. Halfway down, he spotted the ATV lying on its side, bent around a massive oak. Agent Hough was slumped beside it, one hand pressed to his chest. Ruby was at the man's side, her head swiveling on high alert.

Jackson swept the area with his Glock, moving in a controlled slide down the last few yards. "Hough! Status!"

"Took one in the shoulder," Hough grunted. Blood seeped between his fingers, stark against his rain-soaked jacket. "Nothing vital, I think, but it's bleeding like a bitch."

Jackson dropped to one knee beside him, still scanning for threats. "Where's the girl?"

"I never saw her. It's why I shot at him." Hough leaned his head back and sucked in a sharp breath. "This is fucked up. About half a mile from here, up the west face, I passed the remains of an old cabin."

Jackson knew exactly what he was talking about. The makeshift structure looked a hundred years old, constructed of fallen timbers, mud, and grass. Few people knew of its existence because it was in some particularly rough terrain, well away from any of the public trails.

"Someone's using it," Hough said through gritted teeth. "I considered using it as my hideaway, right up until I saw sleeping bags and other camping gear inside."

"Bags?" Jackson asked. "As in, more than one?"

"I think we're dealing with two unsubs. I think the ATV was a decoy, giving his partner a chance to escape with the girl. If I had to wager, I'd guess that's where they're going to meet up."

"Did you see what happened to the driver?" Jackson glanced at Hough—his breathing was ragged, his eyelids heavy. He was fading fast.

Hough nodded, pointing towards the northwest. "He ran off, likely making his way to the cabin." He half chuckled. "Well, limped off is more accurate. His leg was messed up pretty good in the crash. He wasn't moving too well. I'm guessing you'll have no trouble catching up to him."

"Not until I get you patched up," Jackson said. He unslung his rifle and shrugged his backpack off his shoulders.

Hough grabbed his wrist. "You got a first aid kit in there?"

"Yes," Jackson said. "Of course I do."

"Leave it. I'll manage." His grip was already weakening. "Get these bastards. But listen... there's something else, in the cabin. I saw multiple rifles stacked against the wall. Whoever these guys are, they're not going to go quietly."

"I'm going to pack the wound first," Jackson said. "You're in no condition—"

A flash of lightning lit up the area. On the back of the ATV was what looked like a large blue bag. A tarp maybe. Risking being seen, Jackson pulled out his flashlight and opened the first aid kit. He grabbed a wad of gauze and shined the light on the bullet wound. Hough was right. It was unlikely it hit anything vital, but he wouldn't be using that arm anytime soon.

"This is going to hurt," Jackson said as he rammed the gauze into the hole. Hough released a silent scream through gritted teeth. "Press on it. Hard. I'll be right back."

Hough's breath came fast and shallow, his fingers twitching uselessly against the wound.

"Stay with me, brother." Jackson pressed down harder on the gauze, drawing a ragged grunt from Hough. "I need you awake."

Hough's eyes flickered. "Go. I'll be fine."

He was lying. The bullet wouldn't kill him, but the blood loss, the cold, the storm? That would.

"I'm not leaving you like this." He turned his face into the driving rain, doing his best to calm his pounding pulse. "If I can't get you some shelter, you're going to go into shock and die." An idea came to mind. It wasn't ideal, but he saw no alternative.

Jackson moved to the back of the ATV. He unhooked two bungee cords and grabbed the tarp. As he unfurled it, a second fell to the ground and blew away in the wind.

A sharp dread curled deep in his stomach. These weren't for covering gear. They were for the aunt and uncle.

They weren't just taking the kid. They were tying up loose ends.

Jackson rushed back to Hough and wrapped him in the tarp. "Keep your head covered, completely covered if you can manage it. This storm's coming, and when it gets here, the temperature is going to drop. You need to stay warm. Do you hear me?"

Hough nodded and Jackson pulled the tarp over his head. Blowing out a slow breath, he packed his first aid kit, shouldered his pack, and slung his rifle. After stowing his flashlight, he unclipped his radio.

"Brooks?" Frost's voice crackled. "What's happening out there? Is Hough with you?"

"Hough's been shot," Jackson said back, keeping his voice low. "I've done my best to pack the wound and keep him dry, but he needs immediate medical attention. Where's Billingsley?"

"She's heading your way," Frost said. "She's a half mile southeast of your position. I'm sorry, but there's no way of getting medical help to you. Not in this storm."

"Then have her come here. Hough needs someone to watch over him. There are two unsubs. One's injured, and I'm going after him. The other likely still has the child and is headed for an old cabin on the western side of the mountain."

"Understood," Frost replied. "Good luck."

Jackson tightened his grip on his rifle. He wouldn't need luck. He needed speed.

Chapter Eight

One Down

Rain hammered down in icy sheets. Jackson flicked on his flashlight, the beam slicing through the dark. A single boot print stood out in the mud—deep, fresh, and dragging.

"Ruby, here." He crouched beside the print, positioning the light to give her the best view. The Golden Retriever pressed her nose to the ground, taking in the scent. Her entire body tensed as she processed the information, tail rigid, ears forward.

Jackson raised his collar and zipped his jacket as high as it would go. The temperature was dropping fast, just as he'd feared. He hoped the tarp would be enough to keep Hough warm. Billingsley would likely join him, adding her body heat to his.

It's been ages since I laid next to a warm body.

Thunder rolled across the mountainside, closer now.

Another flash of lightning tore through the sky. Seven seconds later, thunder detonated across the mountainside, shaking the earth. The storm was intensifying, threatening to wash away the trail. Jackson looked up the side of the mountain. A flash flood was a real possibility. They were nearly out of time.

"Find him," Jackson commanded.

Ruby surged forward, nose low to the ground. Her usual fluid movement was gone, replaced by the focused intensity of a working dog on a mission. He risked using the flashlight, doing his best to keep her in sight. She weaved between the trees, moving steadily uphill.

"Easy," Jackson called as she started to pull ahead. She slowed immediately, though he could see the tension in every line of her body. She wanted to run, to chase, but she understood the command. In this weather, in this darkness, they needed to stay together.

Jackson kept his Glock ready, sweeping the beam of his flashlight in controlled arcs as they moved. The unsub was injured, desperate, and armed—a dangerous combination. Every shadow could be a threat, every tree a potential ambush site.

They climbed steadily, working their way through dense mountain laurel and fallen trees. The wind howled through the canopy, a constant roar that made it impossible to hear anything beyond a few feet. Rain stung Jackson's face, and his wet clothes clung to his skin. His boots squelched with every step, but he pushed the discomfort aside. Somewhere ahead was a man who was willing to abduct a child, to kill innocent strangers, and who'd shot a federal agent. Nothing else mattered.

Ruby stopped abruptly, her head rising from the ground. Her ears twitched, rotating like radar dishes as she processed information that Jackson couldn't perceive. He killed the flashlight immediately, letting his eyes adjust to the darkness.

A flash of lightning split the sky, turning night into day for a fraction of a second. In that instant, Jackson saw him—a figure about fifty yards ahead, leaning against a tree. The man had a pistol in his hand, head turning frantically as he tried to get his bearings in the storm.

Jackson's pulse thundered against his ribs. He could send Ruby in and end this right now, but at what cost?

She quivered beside him, her whole body coiled like a spring. One command, and she'd be on the abductor. But in this storm, with the unsub armed and twitchy, one bad shot could end her.

He could take the shot himself. Even in these conditions, at this range, he was confident he could make it. But they needed this man alive. He might be their only lead to finding Peggy and his partner. It was only a theory that he was heading to the cabin.

That left announcing himself—but doing it from this distance was asking to get shot. The wind might possibly mask his location, carry his voice away, giving the unsub misleading information.

"Easy," he whispered to Ruby, though she hadn't moved. "With me."

They began moving forward, using trees for cover. The darkness and rain worked in their favor now, masking their approach as they closed the distance. Forty yards. Then thirty. The unsub was still there, still scanning the forest around him. His leg was clearly injured, using the tree for support.

At twenty yards, Jackson made his decision. He clicked on his flashlight, aiming the beam directly at the man's face.

"FBI! Drop your weapon!"

The unsub spun with surprising speed, firing three shots in rapid succession. Two slammed into the tree beside Jackson. The third whizzed past his ear, close enough for him to feel the air shift.

"Ruby, take him!" The command tore from Jackson's throat before he could think twice. The Golden Retriever launched forward like a missile, her powerful legs eating up the distance between her and the target.

Another flash of lightning illuminated the scene. Time seemed to slow as Jackson saw the unsub pivot, gun hand swinging down to track Ruby's charge. In that frozen moment, Jackson could see everything with horrific clarity—the man's finger tightening on the trigger, Ruby's form stretched out in mid-leap, the rain suspended like diamonds in the electric light.

Jackson's instincts fired before his mind could catch up. He squeezed the trigger—once, twice, three times.

The night erupted with sound. The muzzle flash lit up the rain, turning falling drops into frozen silver spears.

The unsub jerked backward. His gun fell from limp fingers. Ruby was on him a fraction of a second later, her teeth finding his throat with trained precision.

"Ruby, off!" Jackson advanced, his weapon still trained on the target. "Off!"

Ruby released her hold and backed away but remained coiled and ready. Jackson approached cautiously, flashlight beam cutting through the rain. The unsub lay motionless, eyes open and unseeing. Three dark holes formed a tight grouping over his heart, each shot expertly placed. His shot. His decision. His kill.

His Glock felt alien in his hand now, like it didn't belong there. He lowered it slowly, his arms suddenly leaden. The rain hammered down around him, but he barely felt it. He had trained for this moment countless times, qualified on the range, and ran through every scenario. But nothing had prepared him for the finality of it. For the burden of knowing he had ended a human life.

The man had been evil. He had shot Hough, tried to steal a child, and would have killed Ruby without hesitation. But he had still been human. And now, he was nothing.

Ruby whined softly and pressed against his leg, pulling him back to the present. Her fur was soaked, but her eyes were bright and alert as she looked up at him. She didn't understand his hesitation. To her, this had been simple—a threat eliminated, her partner protected, the mission continuing.

Jackson took a deep breath, forcing himself to focus. This wasn't over. Somewhere on this mountain, Peggy was still in danger. The second unsub was still out there. He could process his feelings later. Right now, he had a job to finish.

He keyed his radio. "Frost, this is Brooks. Suspect down." His voice felt hollow in his own ears.

He took a breath, steadied himself. "Mark my location for retrieval. I'm heading for the cabin. The girl is still out there."

The radio crackled with Frost's reply, but Jackson was already moving. Ruby trotted at his side, her tail high.

No more hesitation. No more doubt. The job wasn't done.

Behind them, the unsub's lifeless body lay on the ground, the rain pounding down on it, washing away its sins.

Chapter Nine

The Cabin

The weather grew more violent as Jackson and Ruby picked their way through the darkness. Wind howled through the trees, bending them at unnatural angles. Every few minutes, lightning illuminated their path, casting strange, foreboding shadows across the mountainside. In those brief moments of clarity, Jackson could see the toll the weather was taking on the forest—broken branches littered the ground, and small rivulets of water carved new paths down the slope.

Ruby stayed close, her wet fur brushing against his leg with each step. The rain had likely washed away any scent trail, but she seemed to understand where they were headed. Her head remained high, ears constantly moving, trying to catch any sound through the relentless fury.

The land sloped sharply upward, forcing Jackson to brace against the incline. Trees clustered thickly ahead, their gnarled branches clawing at the wind. Then, through the whipping rain, the cabin emerged... dark, angular, and somehow wrong against the natural chaos of the storm. No light shone from its west-facing window, and the structure looked ready to collapse under nature's fierce assault. Jackson touched Ruby's head, signaling her to stay close as they approached.

He pressed his back against the rough wall beside the southern-side window, taking a moment to steady his breathing. The raging weather would cover any sound they made, but it also meant that they wouldn't hear anyone moving inside. His wet clothes clung to his skin, and rainwater ran down his neck, but he barely noticed. All his focus was on what waited inside that cabin.

He slowly shifted his position, trying to peer through the grimy glass without making himself an obvious target. The interior was pitch black, impossible to make out any details. He debated using his flashlight, but the beam would announce their presence to anyone watching.

Lightning split the sky, its white-hot light bursting through the western window. For a fraction of a second, the cabin's interior lit up like mid-day. Jackson's heart lurched. Peggy lay motionless on the dirt floor, her yellow slicker a bright spot in the darkness. She was alone in his field of view, but the cabin's corners remained in darkness even during the flash.

He moved to the door, Ruby a silent presence beside him. The old wood was swollen with moisture, and he knew opening it would make noise no matter how careful he was. But they were out of options. If Peggy was hurt...

Jackson gripped the crude handle and pulled. The door's rusty hinges had barely begun to creak when the gunshot cracked like a whip, and his world turned to chaos. Wood shattered beside his ear, the impact so close he felt the heat of the bullet's passage. A jagged splinter slashed across his cheek, but there was no time for pain. He yanked the door wide and dove inside. Ruby followed, and the wind slammed the door shut behind them, sealing them in total darkness.

Jackson's pulse pounded against his ribs as he crouched in the darkness, Glock extended, sweeping for threats he couldn't see. The air inside was suffocating, thick with the smell of damp wood and rot. Wind howled outside, hammering the walls, searching for cracks to worm its way in. Rain struck the roof in violent bursts, drowning out all other sounds.

He forced his breath to slow, desperate to control his racing pulse. The shot had come from outside. The girl had been left here deliberately—bait in a trap. The bastard had been waiting for Jackson to move to the door, lining up the kill shot. In any other moment, it would have worked. But the wind had betrayed him. Even at close range, it had thrown the bullet off course.

Jackson's boots pressed into the damp earth as he scanned the shadows. If the shooter had been inside, Ruby would have reacted the second they'd entered. But she hadn't. She hadn't barked. She hadn't growled. She hadn't made a sound.

"Ruby, come," he said in a harsh whisper. Cold dread coiled in his gut. Where was she? Ruby had obeyed every command tonight—except this one. His ears strained through the suffocating dark, but the wind shrieked through the gaps around the door, drowning out everything else. No sound. No movement. Nothing. His grip tightened on his Glock.

"Ruby," he repeated, louder and more forceful.

Lightning split the sky, blinding white against the darkness. A heartbeat later, thunder slammed into the cabin, shaking the walls. Ruby was lying next to Peggy, her head resting on the tiny girl's chest, using her body like a shield.

In the darkness, Peggy screamed. The high-pitched terror in her voice made Jackson's blood curdle. His head and Glock swung to the door, and then to the window. The girl's wails continued, enough to drown out the raging elements outside.

Knowing it was a risk, Jackson turned on the flashlight. Peggy had moved away, pressing her tiny body into the corner. Her eyes were squeezed shut, her arms clutched over her sodden blonde hair.

"Peggy," Jackson said. "We're your friends. Your aunt and uncle sent us to find you."

She didn't look up, keeping her face pressed into Ruby's neck ruff, her whole body shaking with sobs. The wind battered against the cabin's wooden frame, but inside, the little girl had gone utterly still, trapped in her own silence. Jackson crouched lower, instinct urging him to fix this, to make her feel safe, but his training told him the truth—she was still trapped in the horror of her abduction.

"We're going to take you to your mommy and daddy," Jackson whispered against her ear. "Ruby will protect you from the bad men."

Then, so softly he almost didn't hear it... A ragged breath.

"I lost a boot." She had managed to speak between hitching breaths, the words muffled by Ruby's fur.

Jackson's throat tightened. Such a small concern in the middle of all this terror, yet so perfectly childlike. "That's okay," he said softly, reaching into his pack. "I've brought something for you."

He held out the blue bunny, its fur still pristine within the protective evidence bag he had placed her in. Peggy lifted her head just enough to see it, then reached out with one trembling hand to take it. Her other hand never left Ruby's fur, maintaining that desperate grip on safety.

"I'll take it out of the bag, okay?" Jackson said. "Bunnies are more fun when you can pet their fur."

With her hand still extended, and her face half-buried in Ruby's fur, the girl nodded.

Jackson ripped open the bag and handed over the fluffy blue prize.

Peggy snatched it away and clutched it to her chest. She burrowed into Ruby's fur, her small body trembling. "Thank you."

The gunfire ripped through the night—three rapid shots, shattering glass, wood, and the cabin's relative silence. Jackson flinched as something hot and sharp tore across his arm. Wind and rain roared through the gaping hole, turning the cabin into a howling, violent wind tunnel.

Jackson lunged. No thought. No hesitation. Just instinct.

He slammed into Peggy, knocking her over as the shots shredded through the wall. The flashlight slipped from his grip, spinning wildly across the floor, its beam flickering like a dying pulse.

"Ruby, guard," he yelled. The K9 immediately curled her body around Peggy, doing what she could to protect her from danger.

Jackson snatched up the flashlight and extinguished its beam. The cabin was no longer a refuge. It was a death trap.

Chapter Ten

Into the Storm

Another bullet punched through the wall, spraying splinters like shrapnel. Jackson pressed himself flat against the rough-hewn logs, his mind racing. The cabin had seemed like a shelter, but now it was just a box with too many holes. The unsub could take his time, picking his shots, waiting for his quarry to make a mistake. And sooner or later, one of those bullets would find its mark.

Peggy whimpered, still clinging to Ruby. The Golden Retriever stood over her protectively, a low growl rolling through her chest with each gunshot. The dog's ears were forward, tracking sounds that Jackson couldn't hear over the storm's fury.

He needed to move. Needed to act. But how? The cabin's single room offered little cover, and the window and door were obvious kill zones. The unsub would be expecting them to bolt, and he'd be ready if they did.

Lightning flashed, and in that instant, Jackson saw everything with absolute clarity. The rotting walls wouldn't stop a bullet. The unsub could shoot through them at will. Staying here wasn't just dangerous, it was suicide.

But Jackson couldn't take Peggy out into that storm, into the line of fire. The girl was already traumatized, and Ruby... she had done her job. She'd tracked the kidnapper, found Peggy, and now she could serve a different purpose.

Jackson ignited his flashlight, the beam cutting through the suffocating dark. He would leave it for Peggy, so that she wouldn't be alone in the darkness. "Ruby, guard," he commanded softly. The dog's eyes locked with his, understanding in their depths. "Protect her with your life."

Ruby pressed closer to Peggy, her body forming a bastion between the girl and the waiting enemy outside. The child's fingers twisted deeper into the dog's fur, and Jackson saw fresh tears tracking down her face in the dim light.

"Peggy, listen to me," he whispered, keeping his voice even while trying to hide the worry churning in his gut. "Ruby's going to stay with you. She won't let anything happen to you. Do you understand?"

The girl nodded, face half-buried in Ruby's neck ruff. Her small hands clutched both the blue bunny and Ruby's fur, anchoring herself to these small comforts in her world's utter chaos.

"I'm going to make the bad man go away," Jackson continued. "But you have to be brave and stay absolutely still. Can you do that for me?"

Another barely perceptible nod.

Jackson took a deep breath, steeling himself. The storm was reaching its peak now—he could feel it in the way the cabin shuddered, hear it in the screaming wind that tore through the broken window and whistled through the bullet holes. The rain was coming down in sheets so heavy they were almost solid. In a way, that was good. The storm would help conceal his movement, make him harder to track.

But it would also make it nearly impossible to see, to move, to fight.

He checked his Glock's magazine, though he already knew he had fired three shots. The familiar motion helped steady his hands. One more deep breath, then he moved to the door, staying low. He scanned the room, concerned by what he didn't see. There were no weapons in sight, which meant the unsub had an arsenal with him. He racked his brain, trying to recall what the area was like. He might know the state park well, but not well enough to envision where the kidnapper had most likely set himself up.

He placed the flashlight on the ground, pointing it towards the wall. He crept across the room to the door. "I'll be right back," he whispered, just as the world flashed with another bolt of lightning. In the darkness that followed, he pulled open the door a crack and dashed out into hell.

The rain pounded down on Jackson, driving needles of ice through his exposed skin. Wind roared around him, yanking at his clothes, dragging at his balance. He threw himself toward a thick oak, fighting to stay upright.

More lightning forked across the sky. The world flickered between darkness and blinding white, phantoms lunging and retreating with each violent burst.

Mud sucked at his boots as he moved, threatening to pull them off with each step. The ground had turned to soup, treacherous and unstable. Twice he nearly fell, catching himself against trees that swayed alarmingly in the gale. Water ran in sheets down the mountainside, carrying debris and small branches past his feet.

Jackson forced himself forward, using the storm as cover. The unsub had to be close—the shots had come from nearby, and in this weather, no one would risk losing sight of their target. But where? The lightning made it impossible to maintain night vision, and the rain cut visibility to almost nothing.

A jagged streak of lightning sliced through the sky, turning the mountain into a stark, high-contrast nightmare. In that rapid heartbeat, Jackson saw him—a figure, hunched against the wind, moving fast and low through the trees, trying to reposition. Thirty yards away, maybe less. Then blackness swallowed the world again.

Jackson froze, heart hammering. Had the unsub seen him, too?

The afterimage of the figure burned against his vision, a ghost in the dark. He couldn't be sure of the exact position, but he didn't have to be. The bastard was circling, trying to get a better angle on the cabin. That meant he wasn't expecting Jackson to already be outside.

Good. Let him think he still had the upper hand.

Jackson shifted his weight, sinking lower, practically crawling as he moved to cut off the unsub's advances. He needed to get closer before the next lightning flash revealed his own position. He needed to see, needed just one more—

Lightning exploded across the sky, and the world crystallized. The unsub was closer now, fifteen yards at most, using a fallen oak for cover. In that minuscule slice of time, Jackson saw everything: the rifle's sleek outline, the man's rain-slicked jacket, his head turning toward Jackson's position.

Darkness crashed back like a wave. Jackson counted. One. Two—

The crack of the rifle shattered the night. Bark exploded next to his head. Pure instinct hurled him sideways, boots sliding in the mud as he rolled behind a massive pine. His heart hammered against his ribs, but his hand remained stable on the Glock.

The dance had begun. Two predators circling in the dark, weapons raised, waiting for the next flicker of lightning to reveal their enemy. Each blinding flash became a frozen frame, a single heartbeat in their deadly game.

Jackson crept forward, silent, patient. The thunder swallowed his steps, the rain blurred his form—but his prey was just as cunning.

The unsub was good—professional good. He never stayed still long enough for Jackson to get a clean shot, never allowed himself to be silhouetted against the sky. But he was getting desperate. Jackson could sense it in the quickening pace of the rifle shots, in the way the man's movements became less precise, more urgent.

Then Jackson heard it, the distinct click of a magazine being released. It was now or never.

He surged forward, counting steps in his head. The unsub would need three seconds to reload. Lightning strobed, revealing his target crouched behind a waist-high stump. Jackson's finger tightened on the trigger.

The Glock barked twice. The unsub's body jerking from the impact, but he remained upright, staggering, defiant. Jackson fired another pair of rounds, each bullet slamming center-mass. The kidnapper jerked backward, his rifle sagging in his grip. Fingers twitching. Still trying. Still thinking he could win.

Jackson squeezed the trigger again and again. He needed to be certain. Two more rounds slammed home. The unsub gasped—one last, stuttering breath—then crumpled, like a marionette with its strings cut. His rifle clattered against stone in a final, useless protest. Silence followed.

The wind had begun to shift even before the final shot, gusting softer now. The rain lost some of its bite, but the storm was still there, still lingering—just like the ever-tightening knot in Jackson's chest.

He approached carefully, his Glock trained on the still form. But there was no need. The man's eyes stared sightlessly at the roiling sky, six red flowers blooming across his chest. Rainwater and blood mingled in the dirt beneath him, the storm washing them away.

The world tilted sideways. This was the second time he had taken a life, but it didn't make it any easier. Somehow it was worse, weightier. He swallowed down the bile rising into his throat. His head snapped to the cabin at Ruby's bark.

Peggy.

Jackson forced air into his lungs. His hands shook as he stowed his weapon, but his steps were sure as he turned toward the cabin. There would be time later to reflect on what he'd done. Right now, a little girl needed him.

The rain seemed softer somehow as he made his way back, as if the storm itself had spent its fury. Through the broken window, he could see his flashlight's beam still cutting through the darkness, still standing guard over the precious lives within.

Ruby's warning growl greeted him at the door, instantly transforming into a whine of recognition. "Good girl," he whispered, voice rough. "Good girl."

Peggy hadn't moved, still curled against Ruby's protective bulk. But when Jackson knelt beside them, her small hand reached out, fingers trembling. He took it gently into his own.

"The bad man," she whispered, "is he...?"

"He's gone," Jackson said softly. "He can't hurt you anymore. I promise."

She nodded once, tears mixing with her rain-soaked cheeks, then pressed her face back into Ruby's fur. The blue bunny remained clutched tight in her other hand, a talisman against the darkness.

Jackson settled beside them, one hand on Ruby's head, the other on his radio. Soon, he would call it in. There would be questions and reports and the inevitable investigation that followed the taking of a life, two lives, in the line of duty. But for now, he simply sat with them, listening to the storm's retreat, waiting for the exhaustion that was sure to follow once his adrenaline subsided.

The promise was kept. He had made the bad man go away.

The price was still to come.

Chapter Eleven

The After Calm

The storm's fury ebbed like a retreating tide. Wind that had howled through the trees now only whispered, and the torrential rain softened to a continuous patter against the cabin's roof. Jackson stood at the broken window, watching, listening. His body ached with exhaustion, but his mind remained sharp, scanning the forest for any hint of danger. He couldn't shake the idea that the ordeal wasn't over.

Behind him, Ruby's tail thumped softly against the packed-dirt floor. The sound drew his attention back to the corner where the dog still lay curled protectively around Peggy. The girl hadn't moved, her small form pressed tight against Ruby's golden fur, but her eyes were open, tracking his movements.

Jackson pulled his radio from its holster, thumbing the transmit button. Static crackled, then cleared. "Frost, you copy?"

"Reading you loud and clear." Frost's voice came back instantly, tense with concern. "Status?"

"Package secure." Jackson kept his voice balanced, professional. "Subject is…" He paused, glancing toward the darkness beyond the window. "Neutralized."

A beat of silence. "Understood. We've got FBI, local PD, and medical standing by at Cheaha summit welcome center. Can you make it there, or should we come to you?"

Jackson ran through his mental map of the state park. The nearest trail would take them straight to the summit, but after the storm... "I'm coming to you. ETA uncertain. Ground conditions aren't ideal."

"Copy that. We'll be waiting. Frost out."

Jackson tucked the radio away and moved to kneel beside Peggy and Ruby. The girl's clothes were sodden, and he could see her shivering despite Ruby's warmth. One hand twisted into Ruby's fur, the other clutching the blue bunny, lifelines in the storm's aftermath.

"Hey," he said softly, "think you're ready to get out of here?"

Peggy nodded, though uncertainty flickered across her face.

"The trail's pretty rough," he continued, "and it's going to be slippery after all that rain. Would it be okay if I carried you?"

Another nod, smaller this time.

"Ruby," Jackson commanded quietly, "release."

The dog immediately shifted, allowing Jackson to gather Peggy into his arms. She was small—so very small—and her hands immediately gripped his jacket, bunching the material in her small fists. Ruby rose and shook herself, then moved to stand at attention, waiting for orders.

"Let's go," Jackson said, and Ruby trotted to the cabin door, her snout high.

The storm was nearly spent, and the mid-afternoon sun pierced the thinning clouds. The rain fell in a gentle curtain now, and the wind had died to occasional gusts that stirred the dripping branches. But the ground... Jackson's boots sank into the mud as soon as he stepped outside. The trail would be better, he just needed to get there.

Jackson considered his options. The shortest path to Big Foot trail was up the hillside, but with the sodden ground, and the girl in his arms... it wasn't a viable option. It would take them out of their way, but it would be easier on everyone if he moved east to Bunker Loop and took it to the summit.

Ruby moved ahead, her paws finding the surest route, pausing occasionally to look back to ensure they were following. Even with the ground being fairly level, their path to the trail was intersected by small creeks, the water running off the mountainside in muddy rivulets. Jackson's boots slipped more than once, each time forcing him to shift his grip on Peggy to save them from falling.

They had been walking for perhaps fifteen minutes when Peggy's grip on his jacket loosened slightly. Her head, which had been tucked against his shoulder, lifted just enough to watch Ruby's progress.

"What kind of dog is she?" The question came as barely more than a whisper.

"She's a Golden Retriever," Jackson answered, grateful for the break in silence. "One of the smartest dogs you'll ever meet."

"Is she a police dog?"

"Sort of. She's what we call a SAR dog—Search and Rescue. She helps find people who are lost or in trouble."

"Like me?" Peggy's voice trembled slightly.

"Exactly like you. That's how we found you so quickly. Ruby followed your trail all the way to that cabin."

Peggy considered this, her fingers absently stroking the blue bunny's ear. "Does she like treats?"

A smile tugged at Jackson's mouth. "She loves them. Especially peanut butter treats."

"I like peanut butter too," Peggy said. "Mommy makes me peanut butter sandwiches for lunch. She cuts the crusts off and makes them into triangles."

"That sounds pretty good," Jackson said, carefully navigating a particularly treacherous section of trail. "And who's this?" He nodded toward the stuffed rabbit.

"Mr. Hops." Peggy held the bunny up slightly. "Daddy got him for me at the zoo. He's my favorite."

They walked in silence for a while after that, the only sounds their breathing and the constant drip of water from the trees. Jackson could feel Peggy's body gradually relaxing against him, though her grip on his jacket never fully released.

Peggy's lip quivered. She clutched Mr. Hops tighter. Then, so quietly he almost missed it, "But... are you sure? The bad man... he can't come back?"

Jackson stopped, his arms tightening protectively around her. Ruby turned, ears pricked, sensing the shift in mood. The girl was trembling—small, fragile in his grip. He adjusted his hold, just enough to see her wide, fearful eyes.

"I promise, Peggy," he said, his voice even and reassuring. "The bad men are gone. They'll never come back. You're safe now. No one will ever hurt you again."

Peggy's lip quivered. For a second, Jackson thought she might cry, but instead, she only whispered, "Okay."

Then, after a pause, she asked, "Why did they take me?"

Jackson's throat tightened. He hadn't thought about the why. Not until now. Ransom, maybe. But as he replayed the details, something darker settled over him.

The blue tarps he'd found on the ATV weren't meant for her, but for her aunt and uncle. Heat rose in his face, and his pulse quickened.

They were monsters, and they got off easy.

"I don't know," Jackson said. He was doing his best not to let his fury show. "Sometimes, bad people do things that don't make sense, and there's nothing you did to cause it. It wasn't your fault, Peggy. You were very brave."

"Mister?" Peggy said. "Are you okay?" Her brow scrunched up. "I don't know what your name is. My name's Peggy."

"I'm sorry," Jackson said, doing his best to give her a smile. "My name's Jackson. My friends call me Jax."

Peggy tilted her head, thinking. "I like that name," she decided.

Jackson smiled. "Well, Miss Peggy, I like yours too." Widening his eyes in feigned terror, he whispered, "But don't tell my momma I didn't introduce myself properly to you. If she found out, I suspect she'd tan my hide."

Peggy's eyes grew wide. "You mommy spanks you?" She tutted at Jackson and slowly shook her head. "I've never been spanked."

He hiked her higher in his arms, getting her closer to eye level with him. "I'm guessing it's because you're such a good girl that your momma never has a reason to spank you."

An instant blush turned the child's cheeks bright red. "Sometimes I take cookies before dinner. Mommy doesn't know. You won't tell her, will you?"

"It will be our secret," Jackson whispered back conspiratorially. "Just so you know, I sneak cookies before dinner too."

They continued upward, Ruby leading the way through the forest. The rain had stopped entirely now, and the clouds had broken up. The sun's warmth felt good on his face. The one-mile trek up the pea stone trail that led to the welcome center passed quickly. Peggy babbled on and on, telling Jackson about her favorite teachers, and how she loved catching frogs and salamanders. She said her daddy even took her fishing sometimes. The horrors of the day seemed to be behind her, but Jackson was worried for the girl.

The ordeal might be over for Peggy, but she'd likely carry the trauma for years to come. At least... he pushed the thought aside. He didn't want to dwell on how much worse it might have been for her if Ruby hadn't been able to track her, or pick up her scent on the wind. His mind ran through what would come next—the debriefing, the reports, the inevitable investigation into the shooting. But those were problems for later. Right now, his job was simple:

get this child to safety, get her back to her parents, and make sure she knew that the nightmare was truly over.

Ruby's ears suddenly pricked forward, and she quickened her pace. A moment later, Jackson saw it too—the flashing lights of an ambulance. The welcome center was directly ahead of them. He exhaled, long and slow. It was over. No more chasing, no more gunfire, no more nightmares waiting in the dark. The relentless burden on his shoulders, the fear, the urgency, the sheer drive to keep moving... it finally lightened.

"Almost home," Jackson murmured, his voice barely a whisper as he gently shifted Peggy's weight, trying to ease the burden on his arms. He wasn't sure if she was still awake, but he hoped she could hear him, hoped she understood that the worst was behind them.

"Almost home."

Chapter Twelve

The Aftermath

Jackson crested the final rise of the trail, the trees thinning around him. Water droplets still dripped from the branches, pattering softly against the forest floor. The Cheaha Summit Welcome Center stood just beyond the curve, its exterior lights casting a hazy glow through the lingering mist.

The flashing lights of an ambulance and several police vehicles painted the wet ground in pulses of red and blue. Silhouetted figures stood at the ready—FBI agents, uniformed officers, and a handful of first responders. They were waiting for him. Waiting for her.

He adjusted his grip on Peggy, shifting her slightly in his arms. She was quiet now, her head nestled against his chest, her breaths rapid and shallow. The warmth of her small body pressed against him was the only thing grounding him in the moment, keeping his mind from spiraling from everything that had happened.

Ruby walked beside him, her fur damp but her posture alert. As they neared the welcome center, the dog let out a small huff, sensing the shift in atmosphere—the thick tension of expectation.

"Peggy!" Eileen, Peggy's aunt shrieked, her arms outstretched, as she raced from the ambulance. Her husband, Bernie, ran in her wake.

Jackson had barely steadied himself before Eileen reached for her niece, her hands trembling as she smoothed Peggy's damp hair away from her face.

"Oh, sweetheart, we've got you," she whispered, her voice cracking. "We've got you."

Bernie placed a hand on Peggy's back, rubbing it in small circles. His jaw clenched, his eyes rimmed red, but his voice remained calm and composed. "Are you hurt?"

Peggy shook her head, burrowing against Jackson's chest. "M'okay," she mumbled. She turned to her aunt, her little face wrinkled with worry as she displayed her sodden socked foot. "I lost my boot."

Jackson burst out laughing, along with Bernie and Eileen. After everything that had happened, after everything she had endured, Peggy seemed most upset at having lost her pretty pink boot.

"We can't thank you enough," Bernie said, struggling to get the words out. He looked to his wife and the couple immediately embraced, clutching on to each other, overwhelmed by the day's events.

A petite paramedic in a bright yellow rain jacket stepped forward, swiping damp strands of mousy-brown hair from her face. "We need to check on the child." She reached out to take Peggy from Jackson's arms.

"No!" Peggy's tiny voice cracked, raw with sudden panic. Her grip tightened on Jackson's jacket, clutching fistfuls of fabric in her tiny hands. "Don't let me go. Please, don't!"

Jackson's heart clenched. He crouched down until Peggy was eye level with the young paramedic. At six-foot-three, he was well over a foot taller than the EMT. "Peggy, listen to me," he said gently. "This nice lady is here to help you. She just wants to make sure you're okay. Your aunt and uncle will be with you."

Tears welled in her big blue eyes. She shook her head fiercely. "But—" she looked down at Ruby.

"She can stay with you, if you want," Jackson promised. He gave a quick gesture, and the golden retriever immediately sat and looked up at the child. "See? She'll be with you the whole time."

"Would you like me to carry you?" Bernie asked, holding out his arms.

Peggy's grip on Jackson's jacket slackened slightly, her fingers shifting to the dog's fur instead. She chewed her lip, then nodded.

Only then did Jackson carefully relinquish the tiny child. The instant Peggy left his arms, the crash came.

His body, held together by adrenaline and sheer will, began to betray him. His knees wobbled, his shoulders throbbed, and a bone-deep exhaustion settled in. He sucked in a breath, but it barely seemed to reach his lungs. The relentless pressure of the day—the stolen child, the storm, the gunfire—pressed down all at once.

"Let's get her inside," the paramedic said, motioning towards the welcome center. "She needs to be checked for hypothermia."

As they moved toward the ambulance, Peggy looked over her uncle's shoulder, her eyes locking onto Jackson's.

"Will you come too?" she asked, her voice small, uncertain.

Jackson hesitated. He wanted to. He wanted to see her through every step, wanted to make sure she never felt alone for a second. But this was where his role ended.

"I have to talk to some people first," he said, offering her the closest thing to a reassuring smile he could manage. "But I'll see you before you leave. Okay?"

She studied him for a long moment, then nodded. "Okay."

Jackson exhaled slowly, rubbing a hand down his face.

"Brooks," Frost said with a curt nod. "You look like hell." The agent's mannerisms were stoic. His sharp gaze swept over Jackson first, taking in the mud-caked clothes, the bloodstains on his sleeve, and the exhaustion written across his face. Then his eyes flicked back to Peggy and her family, and his entire demeanor changed. Jackson could see the pride in his expression.

Jackson let out a breath that was almost a laugh. "Feel like it too."

Frost's expression softened, just slightly. "Let's get you inside, too. We've got warm blankets and coffee. As soon as you're up to it, we need to talk."

The inside of the welcome center was warm, chasing away the damp chill from outside. Jackson sat at a table with a steaming mug of coffee in front of him. What he really wanted was a gallon of water. He looked over at Peggy who was being examined by the paramedics. She caught his eye and waved. Jackson waved back.

Frost sat across from him, along with SA Billingsley.

"How's Hough?" Jackson asked, his voice cracked unexpectedly.

Billingsley gave a small nod. "Stable. He's already on his way to Birmingham General for treatment." A pause. "He's alive because of you."

Jackson glanced down at his hands, then shook his head. "He's alive because he's too damn stubborn to die."

A ghost of a smile crossed Frost's face before he sat back, his expression shifting to business. "Walk us through it."

Jackson recounted everything, step by step. From following the ATV, to tracking the first unsub through the storm, to finding Peggy, to the gunfight in the woods, where he'd put six rounds into the second kidnapper. His voice was even, clinical. Detached.

But when he finished, the trio sat silent for a long time. Finally, Jackson broke the tension.

"So," he said, as an unexpected nervousness crept through him. "Does Ruby need to retest?"

Frost ran a hand down his face, shaking his head with a quiet laugh. "No, I don't think that will be necessary. It was all a bit unorthodox, but I'd say she's more than exceeded the necessary requirements. Moving forward, I'd like to know more about how she progresses. The two disciplines don't mix, but clearly, Agent Ruby is an exceptional K9."

"Thank you," Jackson said, butterflies fluttering in his stomach. He firmly believed that the combination of SAR and tracking skills were complementary, even if his boss disagreed. "If it's all the same to you, I'd like to take Ruby home. We both need a bath and a good long rest."

"Say your goodbyes, and I'll drive you to your car," Frost said with a grin. "I don't think you're up for another hike."

"Agent Brooks, sir?"

He turned. Peggy's aunt and uncle stood there, their faces drawn, their eyes red-rimmed. But Peggy was between them, clutching Mr. Hops in one arm, her other hand tightly grasping onto Ruby's neck ruff.

"She insisted on seeing you," Eileen said, voice thick with emotion.

Jackson crouched, exhaustion momentarily forgotten. "Hey, kiddo."

Peggy hesitated, tiny fingers still twisted in Ruby's fur. Then, suddenly, she was there—throwing herself into his arms, her small frame trembling against him.

"Thank you," she whispered.

Jackson's breath caught. He closed his eyes, letting the moment sink in. When he finally spoke, his voice was rough.

"Anytime, Peggy."

She pulled back, offering him a shy smile, then turned and walked back to her family.

Jackson watched them go. "Bye, Ruby," she called back over her shoulder. "I love you."

For the first time since this whole nightmare started—since the chase, since the storm, since the gunshots—Jackson let himself believe it was over.

Chapter Thirteen

VCAC

The morning light filtered through the kitchen windows of Jackson's childhood home, casting long shadows across the worn wooden floor. Ruby lay at his feet, her chin resting on his boot, while the familiar sounds and smells of his mother's cooking filled the air. The coffee maker gurgled, bacon sizzled, and the rustle of his father's newspaper provided a comforting backdrop to the quiet morning.

Jackson's mother moved casually about the kitchen, though he could sense her watching him from the corner of her eye. She'd always been good at that—observing without seeming to observe, gathering information while appearing completely focused on other tasks.

His father sat at the head of the table, newspaper creating a barrier between them. Captain James Brooks, twenty-five years with the Florence Police Department, had perfected the art of saying volumes without speaking a word. Right now, his silence spoke of concern, carefully restrained.

The eggs hit the pan with a sharp sizzle. Jackson flinched—just slightly, but enough. His mother paused for a fraction of a second before continuing. Ruby's tail thumped once against the floor, and she pressed closer to his leg.

"More coffee, honey?" His mother's voice was carefully neutral.

"I'm good, Momma." The mug in front of him was still full, gone cold while he stared into its depths.

The newspaper rustled as his father turned a page. "Weather's supposed to clear up today."

Jackson nodded, grateful for the mundane observation. Weather was safe. Weather didn't require him to examine the hollow ache in his chest since that night on the mountain.

His mother set a plate in front of him—eggs, bacon, toast arranged just as she'd done throughout his childhood. The sight of it made his throat tight with an emotion he couldn't name.

"Have you..." she began, then paused, weighing her words. "Have you been able to talk to anyone? About what happened?"

"The department shrink cleared me," Jackson said flatly. "I'm fine."

Another rustle of newspaper. His father's eyes appeared briefly over the top edge, studying him.

"That's not what I asked," his mother said softly.

Jackson pushed back from the table, the chair legs scraping against the floor. "Come on, Ruby. Let's get some air."

The Golden Retriever was on her feet instantly, padding after him as he stepped out onto the back porch. The morning air was cool, carrying the scent of his mother's rose garden and the promise of spring. Jackson descended the steps, his boots leaving prints in the dew-laden grass.

Ruby stayed close, matching his pace as they walked the familiar path around the yard. How many times had he walked this same route as a teenager, working through various problems? How many times had he watched his father do the same thing, silently wrestling with his own difficult days?

The shooting played through his mind again—the flash of lightning, the sound of the Glock, the way the unsub's body had crumpled. He'd done what needed to be done. He knew that. The review board knew that. So why couldn't he shake this feeling?

"Brooks residence."

His father's voice carried from the house, making Jackson turn. Through the kitchen window, he could see his father standing with the phone pressed to his ear, his expression serious. After a moment, he stepped onto the porch.

"Jackson. It's SAC Baldwin."

Something cold settled in Jackson's stomach. He walked back to the house, each step feeling heavier than the last. Ruby pressed against his leg as he took the phone.

"This is Brooks."

"Agent Brooks." Alice Baldwin's voice was crisp, professional. "The investigation into the shooting is complete. You're cleared for duty, effective immediately."

Jackson exhaled slowly, his grip tightening on the phone. Cleared. Just like that. But the ache in his chest didn't vanish, it just settled into a dull presence beneath his ribs. He had done everything right. So why did it still feel like something had been lost?

Baldwin wasn't finished.

"There's something else I'd like to discuss with you," she continued. "Your handling of the kidnapping case was exceptional. The way you and Ruby worked together, the decisions you made under extreme pressure, the compassion you both showed for the child—it's exactly the kind of skill set we need in our Violent Crimes Against Children unit."

Jackson's grip tightened on the phone. "Ma'am?"

"I'd like you to consider joining VCAC. Your experience with tracking, your work with Ruby, and your proven ability to handle high-stress situations make you an ideal candidate."

"I..." Jackson glanced at his parents, who were trying very hard to look like they weren't listening. "I appreciate the offer, but I doubt that I'm built for that kind of work."

"Think about it," Baldwin said. "Come by my office tomorrow. We can discuss it in detail."

After hanging up, Jackson relayed the conversation to his parents. His father's face darkened immediately.

"The Violent Crimes Against Children task force?" His mother's voice was tight with concern. "Jackson, that's not... after everything that's happened..."

The memory of his debriefing resurfaced, dragging Jackson back to one of the worst days of his life.

Jackson leaned back, exhaustion pressing down on him as SAC Baldwin slid a case file across the table.

"The men responsible for Peggy's abduction," Baldwin said, her voice grim, "weren't just opportunists. They were criminals of the worst possible breed."

Jackson flipped open the file. Mugshots of the two deceased suspects stared back at him. One was a low-level trafficker with ties to an interstate child smuggling ring. The other—Jackson's stomach twisted—was a part-time park ranger.

"Paul Grayson," Baldwin continued, tapping the ranger's photo. "Worked at multiple state parks across Alabama, Georgia, and Tennessee. Every year, a few families would vanish, usually in remote areas. No bodies, no ransom demands. Just... gone." She exhaled sharply. "We suspected foul play but never found a common link. Until now."

Jackson's hands clenched the edge of the file. He'd been chasing a kidnapper, but what he'd really found was a serial predator, hidden in plain sight.

"He used his knowledge of the parks," Baldwin went on, "to cover his tracks. He led families into isolated areas, eliminated the adults, and handed the kids off to traffickers like Vincent Hale here." She gestured to the second suspect's photo. "We think Hale was the connection to a larger operation. He and Grayson were supposed to meet at that cabin before we intervened."

Jackson exhaled slowly, nausea curling in his gut. "And the missing families?"

Baldwin's expression darkened. "We've started searching remote areas where Grayson worked. So far, we've recovered three sets of remains."

Silence stretched between them, heavy and suffocating.

Jackson shut the file. He had done what he had set out to do. He had saved Peggy. But now he knew the full scope of what they had uncovered. And how many they hadn't.

"They got off easy," he muttered.

Baldwin's eyes flicked to him, unreadable. "Maybe. But thanks to you and Ruby, their operation is over."

Jackson glanced down at Ruby, who sat at his feet, her steady presence anchoring him. She had saved a life that night. But she had also unearthed years of buried horrors.

Jackson shuddered. He had suffered many sleepless nights after the abduction, plagued by nightmares and what ifs. His therapy sessions had helped, but not entirely.

"Your mother's right," his father said, setting his newspaper aside. "That kind of work takes a toll. The things you see, the cases you work—it changes people."

Jackson dragged a hand through his hair. "I know. I'm not looking to transfer, but..."

He glanced down at Ruby, at the unwavering trust in her eyes, the certainty she carried when everything else felt uncertain. He had sworn to protect people, to bring the lost home. And now—now he had a choice.

"I can't just turn my back if we could help."

His mother gently laid her hand on his chest. "You've always had a good heart, honey. Just like your father. But sometimes, a good heart can lead you places you're not ready to go. Places you can't return from."

Jackson nodded, but his mind was already working through the possibilities. Ruby's tracking abilities, combined with her gentle nature around children—it could make a real difference in the right situations.

The morning sun had risen fully now, burning away the last of the dew. Jackson checked his watch, knowing he needed to head back to Birmingham soon.

"I should get going," he said. Ruby moved in beside him, alert and ready.

His mother hugged him tightly. "Be careful," she whispered, squeezing his arm. "And call if you need anything. Anything at all."

His father's handshake was firm, conveying everything that went unsaid between them. Pride, concern, understanding—it was all there in that simple gesture.

At the door, Jackson paused, looking back at his parents. They'd always been his anchor, his safe harbor when the world got too heavy. But this decision, like the one he'd made that night on the mountain, was his alone to make.

"I'll be okay," he said, almost believing it.

Ruby jumped into the back seat of his truck, settling into her usual spot. As Jackson slipped in behind the wheel, she placed her head on his left shoulder, her whiskers tickling his neck. He scratched behind her ears, earning a contented sigh from his partner.

"Ready, girl?"

Her tail thumped against the seat in response.

As they pulled away from his childhood home, Jackson's mind was already turning toward Birmingham, toward whatever challenges awaited them there. The heaviness in his chest remained, but it had changed—no longer a burden, but a direction. A purpose.

He didn't know if he was ready for what SAC Baldwin was proposing. Maybe he never would be. But out there, beyond the horizon, there would be another trail to follow. Another child waiting in the dark.

And when the time came, he and Ruby would answer that call.

It wouldn't be easy. Nothing worth doing ever was. But they would face it together, one step at a time, one trail at a time, one rescue at a time.

Just like they always had.

Afterword

Thank you so much for reading. I hope you enjoyed the journey as much as I loved writing it.

If you want to be the first to know when the next case drops, join my inner circle for exclusive updates and early alerts on new releases. You can sign up instantly online at:

https://paulmouchet.ca/subscribe

If the story kept you turning the pages, I'd be incredibly grateful if you shared your thoughts in a review. Reviews on **Amazon, Goodreads, and BookBub** help other readers discover my books and allow me to keep writing more stories for you.

Even a few words make a world of difference. Your support means everything.

— Paul/PJ Mouchet

Also By

PJ Mouchet Novels

Brooks & Banks Series (Adult 14+)

Character-driven thrillers filled with high-stakes investigations, intense confrontations, and the human struggles that bind us all.

- Violent Echoes

- Deep Water

- The Crucible

- No Safe Trail

Paul Mouchet Novels

The Last Guardian Series (Adult 14+)

From unwanted outcast to the last Guardian of the Realm. Some paths are easier than others to follow.

- Rosemarked Assassin

- The Olander Legacy

- Realm of Arachnielle

Priest of Titan Series (Young Adult 14+)
Titan called her. The Temple forged her. Gods will fear her.
Life for Kit was difficult, growing up a Nomad human in a Berrat village. At the tender age of eleven, she travelled to a distant kingdom, and joined the Fist of Titan, a temple that worships a foreign god. The Temple priests trained her in the art of war. They taught her to deliver justice. They set her on the path to free their god, Titan. But paths have a way of taking you in unexpected directions and help you to discover things about the world and yourself. They can show you that meddling in the affairs of gods can either save or destroy the world. How can a teenage girl and her eclectic group of friends save the people and still prevent Ragnarök, the end of days?

- Call of Titan

- Hand of Titan

- Hammer of Titan

- Eyes of Titan

- Daemon of Titan

- Wrath of Titan

Fairytale Retellings (Young Adult 12+)
If you enjoy fantasy adventure with a touch of romance, then this is for you.

- Between Land and Sea: A Little Mermaid Retelling